AETERNA PUBLISHING

The Graymouse Family

by

Nellie Mabel Leonard

TABLE OF CONTENTS

GRAYMOUSE FAMILY

CHAPTER I.

THE GRAYMOUSE HOME

Mother Graymouse, with her family lived in a cosy attic which was as snug and comfortable as any good mouse could wish.

Her children were named Limpy-toes, Silver Ears, Buster, Teenty and Tiny, and Baby Squealer. Although they had many faults, upon the whole they were good children and made a happy family.

On pleasant mornings, the sun shone in bright and warm through the dainty cobweb curtains of their east window. In the summer-time, robins and orioles sang sweetly among the green branches of the maple tree which shaded the west window. Even when it stormed, Mother Graymouse and her little ones enjoyed the patter, patter of the rain-drops upon the roof and window-panes. They were thankful for such a good home.

The house in which they lived belonged to a family of giants. There was Mr. Giant, his wife, and two little Giants. The little girl was a pretty child named Ruth, with blue eyes and long yellow curls. Her brother, Robert, looked almost exactly like her, except that his yellow curls were shorter, he wore bigger boots that made more noise, and instead of playing with dolls and tea-sets he liked balls and bats and air-rifles.

After Mr. Giant had fitted up half of the attic for his children's play-room, life was much jollier for the little Graymouses. The steam heat from the play-room came through the cracks and made their home as warm as toast.

Limpy-toes and Silver Ears worked busily away until there were three holes through which they could steal softly in and watch Ruth and Robert at their play.

Since Christmas the attic had become a merry, noisy place.

"I wonder how those young Giants manage to make such a racket?" grumbled Mother Graymouse. "I've been trying for an hour to rock Baby Squealer to sleep and the poor dear is wide awake now. Such a din, I've seldom heard."

"It's their Christmas presents, Mammy," replied Silver Ears. "Ruth has a toy piano."

"And Robert blows his new cornet and beats his drum," finished Limpy-toes.

"He must like to work so hard," drawled Buster.

"Oh, it's jolly fun!" cried Tiny.

"It's jolly fun," echoed her twin Teenty.

"Maybe it is," said Mother Graymouse, "but I'd like to chew a hole in those toys that would let out all the noise. With their racket and Squealer's howling, I'm almost crazy. Here, Silver Ears, sit by the cradle and amuse the baby. I must try to find something for our supper. Buster, I want you to help the twins set the dishes on the table while I am gone. Don't shirk now. Even if Limpy-toes is so lame, he helps me far more than you do. See the nice dish he is carving out of a walnut shell for me. I shall cook his favorite pudding in it to-morrow as a reward for his patient toil. Aren't you ashamed to be idle when your poor crippled brother tries so hard to help his mother? Now be good children and don't quarrel." She slipped on her gray coat and the bonnet trimmed with blue ribbons and whisked out of sight down a hole in one corner of the attic floor.

Silver Ears left little Squealer to cry himself to sleep while she stood on tiptoe before the old cracked looking-glass and tied a pink ribbon in a bow under her chin.

"Where did you get that ribbon, Miss Prinky?" asked Buster.

"In the play-room," laughed Silver Ears. "It used to belong to the doll, but now it belongs to me."

"You look very sweet, Silvy," lisped Tiny.

"You're sweet, Silvy," chimed in Teenty.

Silver Ears made them a charming bow. "I thank you, twinnies! I'll bring you both something nice from the play-room some day. Now hurry! Mammy will soon return and you haven't even laid the table-cloth. Run and get the spoons from the cupboard, Buster, or I'll tell Mammy to put you to bed without any supper. Oh, that baby! Can't you jiggle the cradle, Limpy-toes, while you finish digging out the dish?"

Mother Graymouse looked very sober when she came home. She took a cracker and some stale cake crumbs from her pocket.

"This is all I could get to-night, my dears," she explained sadly. "That wicked Thomas Cat is prowling about and I had to be careful. It is snowing and the drifts are very deep, so I did not dare go across the street to the store. Ah well, we shall not starve."

"Never mind, Mammy," said Limpy-toes. "Crackers and cake crumbs are nice."

"By and by it will be summer, Mammy, and then we can all go out to hunt for food," added Silver Ears cheerfully.

"But I want some cheese with my cracker," whimpered Buster.

"When your poor Daddy was alive, we had cheese or meat for every meal. He was a wonderful provider. And so clever! What other family has a cradle like ours? And my rocking-chair--I'm quite proud of it. He made 'em all,--every stick of furniture we have, with his own clever paws. Poor Daddy, I miss him so! It is a cold world for a lone widow to be left in with six small children." Mother Graymouse sighed and wiped a tear away with her handkerchief.

The five little mice tiptoed to their places at the table very quietly, for Limpy-toes had rocked Baby Squealer to sleep at last. They ate their supper in silence. Only Tiny and Teenty whispered and giggled softly to each other.

Suddenly there was a great scrambling and scratching outside.

"It is Uncle Squeaky!" cried Limpy-toes.

"He's coming up the elevator," decided Silver Ears.

"Oh, how lovely to have a visit from Uncle Squeaky on a snow-stormy night!" and the twins ran a race to the attic entrance.

"Boo-hoo!" cried Baby Squealer.

CHAPTER II.

UNCLE SQUEAKY

The little Graymouse children greeted Uncle Squeaky gleefully. Silver Ears took his fur cap and cane, Limpy-toes hung up his great-coat, and the twins captured both his kindly paws and danced back to the chimney corner with him.

Buster was such a fat, lazy fellow that he just sat upon his little stool and waited for his uncle to come to him.

"Howdy do, Uncle Squeaky?" he said as the others drew their little red-painted stools into a half circle before Uncle Squeaky's arm-chair. "Have you any peppermints in your pocket?"

"And will you please tell us a real exciting story?" begged Silver Ears.

Uncle Squeaky laughed until tiny wrinkles came all around his twinkling, black eyes and he looked ever so pleasant.

"Just listen to that, Ma Graymouse!" he cried.

"Just listen to that! One would think I was a walking candy store and a story book, all in one. Very sorry, Buster Boy, but I haven't a single peppermint in my pocket. I think you ought not to eat so much candy. You are too fat, already. As for stories, you kiddies have heard every tale that this old gray head holds, time and time again."

He watched the five sober little faces as they sat upon their red-painted stools with their paws folded primly in their laps. Then he winked slyly at Mother Graymouse. "Oh, well, if you are going to feel as bad as all that, perhaps I might manage to tell you one more story," he chuckled. "But I think Silver Ears will hardly call it exciting. And I wonder if you little folk could make some checkermints do?"

He drew forth a handful of pink candies from his pocket and gave them three apiece.

"Bless my stars, how that little Squealer does squeal! Here, Ma Graymouse, stuff his mouth with this candy and I will begin my story:"

"Once upon a time, away up in an attic, so high that it made their fat old uncle puff to climb up to their dwelling, there lived a widow and her six children. Their father met

4

a sad death a short time ago and so her children had to be very brave and work hard to help their dear mother."

"Sniff! Sniff!" went Mother Graymouse behind her handkerchief.

"Boo-hoo!" cried Baby Squealer.

Uncle Squeaky passed Mother Graymouse another checkermint for the baby and went on with his story:

"The oldest son was much like his Daddy, very wise and clever at making things. He was somewhat lame as he had lost the toes of one foot in a trap when he was a small mouse, too small to be wise."

"Limpy-toes!" they cried in a chorus.

"And a great comfort he is, to be sure," put in Mother Graymouse heartily.

"And there was a pretty daughter who loved bright ribbons and spent quite a good deal of time dancing before the looking-glass. But she was good-natured and helpful, with all her gay ways and dainty habits, and every one who knew her loved her."

"Silver Ears, of course!" shouted the others.

"The third little fellow resembled his Grand-daddy Whiskers," continued Uncle Squeaky. "He was fat as a butter ball, so he could not squeeze through holes to hunt for food with the others. He ate so many goodies that he was too tired to do much work, so he had to sit on his little red stool most of the time. But he could sometimes sing the baby to sleep, which was a great blessing. He was a sweet singer and now he is going to sing us a song. Wake up, Buster Boy, and give us a right good tune."

Buster blinked sleepily.

"It is rather warm in this chimney corner," excused Mother Graymouse. "Now, Buster, sing your newest song for Uncle Squeaky; that's a good child."

Buster rubbed his sleepy eyes and began:

"Cheese oh! Merry oh!
Apple pie and cream;
Cheese oh! Merry oh!
Pudding that's a dream.

"Heigh oh! Merry oh!
Spice cake's very nice;
Heigh oh! Merry oh!
We are happy mice."

"A voice just like his poor Daddy's," sighed Mother Graymouse, "and so he is a comfort, too."

"Then there was a pair of twins," resumed Uncle Squeaky. "The two of 'em wouldn't make one good sized mouse. But it did not take much stuff for their dresses and they could steal through the tiniest, teentiest holes, which was often very handy for the whole family."

How they all clapped for Tiny and Teenty!

"Hush!" cautioned Mother Graymouse. "If we make too much noise, the Giant may be angry and turn us out of our cosy home."

"Then there was a small baby; he was rightly named Squealer," added Uncle Squeaky dryly. "Well, one stormy night when the snow was packed against the windows so you couldn't even peep out, their old uncle made them a visit. He reminded them that once again it was New Year's Eve." He paused solemnly.

"And so we must make new resolutions," smiled Silver Ears.

"Very good," agreed Uncle Squeaky. "Suppose you begin."

"I will obey my mother," said Silver Ears.

"I will try to take poor Daddy's place," said Limpy-toes.

"I will mind the baby," said Tiny.

"I will mind baby, too," said Teenty.

"Your turn, Buster," reminded Uncle Squeaky.

"I will try to wake up mornings," said Buster.

"And not eat so much, my boy. And do a little more work; it is good exercise," advised Uncle Squeaky in a rather severe tone.

"Now that is fine. Good little mice are always obedient and helpful. I think, Ma Graymouse, that you ought to be very happy and contented this year with such dutiful kiddies. Now it is getting late. I must tell you the good news which was my real errand, and then be gone. Granny and Grand-daddy Whiskers have met with great good fortune. They have moved up one flight into the pantry closet. They say the air there is very fine--all sorts of delicious odors. And food! Why, it is hard to choose the bill of fare, there's so many goodies laying around! Granny wishes you to visit her and bring all the kiddies,--especially Buster," he grinned. "Good night. A happy New Year to you all!"

"Happy New Year, Uncle Squeaky!" they called in chorus. "Bring your fiddle next time, uncle," coaxed Silver Ears, as he pulled his fur cap down snugly.

"And don't forget the checkermints," drawled Buster from his little red stool.

CHAPTER III.

TREASURES FROM THE PLAY-ROOM

Tiny and Teenty were inquisitive little twins. One fine day, when Mother Graymouse had taken Baby Squealer down cellar to call upon Aunt and Uncle Squeaky, and Limpy-toes had been sent to the store across the street, they planned a pleasure trip of their own.

"Silvy and Limpy-toes often visit the playroom and have a lovely time," whispered Tiny. "Let's go, you and I."

"Let's go!" agreed Teenty, clapping her paws.

"We'll stay just as long as we wish," planned Tiny.

"So we will. It will be good fun," answered Teenty.

Silver Ears heard them whispering and giggling together, but she was busy making herself a blue velvet hood from some pieces that Mother Graymouse had found in an old trunk. So she never noticed when Tiny and Teenty slipped through a hole that led to the play-room.

"Oh, isn't it grand to come all by ourselves!" whispered Tiny.

"Isn't it grand!" echoed Teenty.

"Mammy Graymouse will think we are old enough to look out for ourselves if only we can find something nice to take home to her," went on Tiny. "Oh, see, Teenty, they haven't thrown away their Christmas tree, yet! I smell goodies. Why, it is pop-corn! But I never saw it growing on a string before. Hurry and pull it off before the young giants come."

Tiny and Teenty cut the strings of pop-corn with their sharp teeth and they fell softly to the carpet.

All at once, the door flew open and in ran Ruth and Robert Giant.

Tiny and Teenty scrambled out of sight under the sofa pillows and sat tremblingly holding each other's cold little paws, while their hearts went thumpity-thump!

8

"Norah must throw out this tree to-day," said Ruth Giant. "It has stood here nearly a month. The hemlock is falling all over the carpet."

"Even the pop-corn is falling," laughed Robert. "I am going to draw a picture of the tree and color it with my new paints."

"And I will read another chapter in my book before papa comes back with the auto."

It was so still in the play-room that the poor scared twins under the pillows were afraid the Giant children would hear their hearts beating pitty-pat! pitty-pat! It seemed a long, long time before Maid Norah's freckly face appeared in the doorway.

"Your pa says you're to hurry if you want to ride in the auto with him," she announced.

Flying footsteps, slamming doors, and then the play-room was deserted.

Tiny and Teenty crept shyly from their hiding-place, feeling very stiff.

"Oh, see, Teenty!" cried Tiny. "There's a bag of Christmas candy away up in the tree. The young Giants did not find it." Up among the branches she scrambled, almost to the tip-top of the tall tree.

Her sharp white teeth cut the string arid with a bang, down fell their prize. Then Tiny swung herself nimbly to the floor.

"Such a lot of candy! Won't Buster grin," laughed Tiny as she caught up a string of pop-corn and started for home.

Teenty took another string and followed after her sister.

"See, Silvy, what a nice lot of pop-corn we have brought," said Tiny.

"See my nice pop-corn, too," echoed Teenty.

"Why, isn't that lovely!" cried Silver Ears. "I will put it away safely on the cupboard shelf and perhaps Mammy will make us a pop-corn pudding."

"And, Silvy," went on Tiny eagerly, "there's a bag of candy, oh, a very big bag of candy, on the play-room floor."

"It's a very big bag of candy," said Teenty.

Buster pricked up his ears. "Shall I help you bring it home?" he offered. "Oh, please do. And Silvy, too, for it's a real giant bag of candy," explained Tiny, excitedly.

So they all four marched into the play-room and tugged and tugged until they had pulled the candy bag close to the biggest hole. But oh dear me! Even the biggest hole was ever so much too small.

Silver Ears sat down and scratched her head thoughtfully. "How shall we ever manage to get it home?" she asked.

"I know," planned Buster. "Let's eat it right here. That is a nice easy way."

"Oh, no," said Silver Ears. "The Giants might come back, or old Tom. Besides, I want Limpy-toes and Squealer and Mammy to share our goodies. We will untie the string and take out the candies. Buster and Tiny must go through the hole and Teenty and I will push the candies through, one piece at a time."

"That is hard work," grumbled Buster. "My way was ever so much easier."

Silver Ears gave the fat, lazy, little fellow a shove that sent him squealing through the hole.

Tiny followed quickly after. Soon the four little mice were busy shovelling candy. It was rather hard work; "almost as bad as shovelling coal into a bin," Buster thought.

"Silvy, make Buster help me," complained Tiny. "He is just sucking the candy off his paws and I'm most buried up."

"Well, my paws are all sticky," drawled Buster.

"Get to work, Buster, and help Tiny," called Silver Ears, sharply, "or I'll come through the hole and shake you till you'll see stars."

At last every stick of the pretty colored candy was pushed through into the Graymouse side of the attic. Teenty frisked through and Silver Ears danced after her, with the candy bag rolled in a little bundle under one arm.

When Mother Graymouse came home just at dusk, after a delightful visit with Aunt Squeaky and all the little Cousin Squeakies, a fine surprise awaited her.

Limpy-toes had returned from the store with plenty of cheese, a slice of boiled ham and some cute little oyster crackers. Silver Ears and the twins had set the table. At each place they had laid a stick of red and white striped candy.

The cupboard door was ajar, and even before Mother Graymouse had put Baby Squealer in his cradle, or taken off her bonnet, she caught sight of the heap of Christmas candies and the popcorn, which looked like a white snow-bank upon the cupboard shelf.

"Sniff! Sniff!" Out came Mammy's handkerchief as she sank into her rocking chair, bonnet, baby and all.

"Boo-hoo!" cried Baby Squealer.

The five little mice looked dismayed.

"What is the trouble now, Mammy?" asked Silver Ears, sadly. "We thought you would be glad. Just see this candy bag. Won't it make a nice shopping bag for you if we make it smaller?"

Mother Graymouse wiped her eyes.

"And so I am glad, my dear Silvy," she smiled. "Did ever a poor widow mouse have such good, helpful children? When I'm sad, I cry. And when I'm glad, I cry, also. Your poor Daddy used to think it very queer. But never mind, my dears. Bring your little stools and we will eat this splendid supper before the tea gets cold."

CHAPTER IV.

MOTHER GRAYMOUSE KEEPS SCHOOL

Silver Ears was very angry and excited one morning when she returned from a visit to the play-room. Her eyes were pink and swollen from crying as she sat beside Squealer in the chimney corner.

"She is a hateful old Norah, Mammy," she burst out at last. "Ruth Giant wants me to be her little pet mouse. I heard her tell Robert. And she tossed me the nicest bit of cake I ever tasted. It was frosted and stuffed with strawberry jam.

"Then that horrid old Norah Maid came in and shoo-ed me with her broom. I hid under the doll's bed. You wouldn't believe the bad things that freckly-faced Norah said. She told Ruth Giant that she wasn't going to have nasty little mice around, running up her skirts, not if she knew it. She stuck her snubby nose up in the air and said it seemed as if the room smelled mousey. Then when I started to run home, because I couldn't listen to such talk a minute longer, she cried--'There he goes now, Miss Ruth! The nasty, thieving, little beast! If there's a creature I can't abide, it's a mouse, to be sure!'

"I'm not a nasty little beast, am I, Mammy? I have a nice warm bath every Saturday night."

"Every Saturday night, the whole six of you," agreed Mother Graymouse wagging her head proudly. "And what could a body ask more of a neat mother mouse with a big family?"

"The Giants have a bath every morning," said Limpy-toes. "Granny Whiskers says so, and of course Granny knows."

"A bath every morning!" cried Silver Ears. "Just think of that."

"Just imagine it!" drawled Buster.

"Well, they must be very dirty children," decided Mother Graymouse. "A bath every morning! I'd be ashamed if my children could not keep clean longer than that. Ruth Giant isn't a bit cleaner, sweeter, nor daintier than my pretty Silver Ears, if I do say so, as shouldn't."

"I'm not a thief either, Mammy," sobbed Silver Ears.

"When that Maid Norah goes about killing flies by the dozens, does she call herself a murderer?" demanded Mother Graymouse with indignation. "When that old black Tom gobbles up an innocent mouse for his supper, does she call him a murdering beast? Neither are we thieves," went on Mother Graymouse hotly. "Even mice must live, and unless we eat we will surely die. It is very ill-natured of the Giants to begrudge us the few poor scraps that we are able to pick up. But don't ever let me hear of your eating any cake again, Silver Ears, even if it is stuffed with jam, without first showing it to me," she finished in a severe tone.

"But, Mammy, I'm sure Ruth Giant would not give me cake that was not fit to eat."

Then Mother Graymouse drew up the five little red-painted stools in a row. She sat down before them in her rocking chair with little squirming Squealer upon her knees. She gave him a stick of pink candy to suck, so he would stop squealing while she talked.

"It is very painful," she began slowly, "but I see that I must teach you some lessons this morning. Sit on your little stools and come to order for school. Buster, you sit up straight and pay attention. Now listen every one.

"E--n--e--m--y. Now spell it after me."

"E--n--e--m--y!" piped five shrill little voices.

"Who can tell me what an enemy is?"

Buster waved his paw wildly.

"Something good to eat, Mammy," he answered, smacking his fat little chops.

"I fear, Buster, that I must make a dunce cap for you," said his mother, trying hard not to smile.

"An enemy is a trap that pinches off toes," answered Limpy-toes.

"That cross old Norah is an enemy," decided Silver Ears. "But Ruth Giant is not an enemy."

"Maybe not; maybe not," returned Mother Graymouse. "But I mistrust all the other Giants. So take care, my dears.

"An enemy is anything that will harm us. Traps are our enemies. Some traps look like wire cages with a nice smelly bit of toasted cheese inside. But the silly mouse

13

who enters the cage will only be let out when there is a cruel cat waiting outside to pounce upon him. There are many kinds of traps, but they are all wicked enemies. So beware, my dears.

"Cats are our enemies. You have all seen that cruel old Thomas Cat, the black imp, with brass eyes that shine in the dark like automobile lamps. His teeth are sharp and strong; his claws are like ugly needles. Never take any chances when he is around, my dears.

"The Giants are our worst enemies. They set the traps to catch us; they keep the cat to eat us. Often they try to poison us. That is the reason, Silvy, why you must never eat Ruth Giant's cake until I have seen it.

"Your poor Daddy ate a cracker one day, which was spread with salmon and rat poison. It was the cause of his untimely death. 'Water, water, water!' he moaned. Oh, I shall never forget how he suffered! I helped him down to the pond and found a hole in the ice where he could get water. But he grew worse as soon as he drank. Poor Daddy! And so he died out there in the cold winter weather. Sniff! Sniff! This has been a painful task, but you must remember every word I've spoken this morning. Now for our review lesson."

"E--n--e--m--y, enemy," she spelled.

"E--n--e--m--y, enemy," chanted five obedient mice.

"T--r--a--p, trap," went on Mother Graymouse.

"T--r--a--p, trap," echoed her scholars.

"C--a--t, cat," she continued firmly.

"C--a--t, cat," shrilled all five.

"P--o--i--s--o--n, poison; that is the last word."

"P--o--i--s--o--n, poison," finished the tired little scholars with a sigh.

"Very good," smiled Mother Graymouse. "Very good, indeed! School is dismissed. You may run out and play."

Buster waved his paw high.

"Please, Mammy, I've made a new song. May I sing it now?"

14

"We shall all be delighted. Hush, hush, Squealer, while your clever brother sings to us."

Buster folded his paws in his lap and sang very sweetly:

"Traps are our enemies,
Old Tom Cats, too;
Watch out for Norah's broom,
When she cries Shoo!

"Although the cheese smells nice,
Nibble it not;
Wise little mice you see,
Ne'er will be caught."

"Charming!" cried Mother Graymouse, and all the little Graymouse children clapped their tiny paws.

"I think we will learn it for our bed-time song," decided Mother Graymouse. "It will help you remember the lessons I have taught you to-day."

CHAPTER V.

LIMPY-TOES IS LOST

"May Limpy-toes, Buster and I visit our cousins to-day, Mammy?" asked Silver Ears one bright morning.

"If you will be careful and remember all I have told you. Be sure to come home before dark." The three little mice trotted bravely away. They went down their elevator, then crawled through a dark subway, until they came to the warm cellar where Uncle Squeaky and his family lived. Aunt and Uncle Squeaky had gone to the city, but all the cousins--Dot, Scamper, Wink and Wiggle, were at home. They were very glad to see them. "Mother left us a nice lunch and we will have a picnic together," planned Dot. Dot and Silver Ears looked almost exactly alike. A stranger could hardly have told them apart. Silver Ears had brought some squares of patch-work to sew. She was making a new quilt for Baby Squealer's cradle.

"Let's sew first," said Silver Ears, "and then we can have fun all the rest of the day."

"All right," agreed Dot. "Pa Squeaky always says, 'Work before play, my dears.' I will finish the silk ties I am hemming for Wink and Wiggle." So the pretty cousins sat down cosily together at their tasks.

Scamper invited Limpy-toes and Buster to the apple closet where they often played. Wink and Wiggle went along also.

"How nice the apples smell," said Buster.

"They taste good, too," answered Scamper. Then the five little mice each chose a red apple to nibble.

"Aren't we glad we came, Limpy-toes?" cried Buster.

"It is good fun," said Limpy-toes. "What is that big yellow thing, Scamper?"

"That's our play-house," cried Wink and Wiggle.

"We made it out of a pumpkin," explained Scamper.

"Just see the windows and doors," said Wink.

"Come inside and see how nice it is," invited Wiggle.

They all took their apples and sat down inside the toy house.

"It is very cunning," said Limpy-toes.

"But it must have been hard work to chew it all out," added Buster.

"It did take a long time," admitted Scamper cheerily, "but it was great sport. We like to make our own playthings."

Then Buster and Limpy-toes had to tell the cousins all about the wonderful toys in the Giant's play-room. It was a long story. By the time it was finished, Dot called them to a nice lunch.

In the afternoon, Uncle Squeaky and his wife returned from the city.

"Bless my stars!" cried Uncle Squeaky, "if here aren't three of the Graymouse kiddies! Glad to see you, my dears."

Aunt Squeaky asked about Mother Graymouse's health and wanted to know all about Baby Squealer and the twins. Then she hurried away to change her best gown for a house dress and put away all the bundles.

Uncle Squeaky took down his fiddle and began to play a jig. "Now, Buster Boy, sing us a song?" he coaxed.

Buster loved to sing; so he made no excuses. He folded his paws just as Mammy had taught him and sang:

"Cheese oh! Merry oh!"

while Uncle Squeaky played softly on the fiddle.

"Sing your newest song, Buster," reminded Silver Ears.

Uncle Squeaky was delighted with "Traps are our enemies."

He made them all stand up in a row and sing it over and over until they knew it by heart.

"A very good lesson in rhyme," said Aunt Squeaky wagging her head approvingly.

It seemed a very short time before it began to grow dark.

"We must start home now," said Silver Ears. "We promised Mammy."

"Good mice always keep their promises," said Uncle Squeaky as he filled their pockets with dried pumpkin seeds and raisins.

When Mother Graymouse, with Squealer and the twins, returned from making Granny Whiskers an afternoon call, she found Silver Ears and Buster setting the tea-table.

"Where is Limpy-toes?" she asked.

"He was here only a few minutes ago," said Silver Ears.

Supper was ready and still Limpy-toes was missing. Mother Graymouse grew uneasy.

"Are you sure he came all the way home from Uncle Squeaky's with you, Silvy?"

"Quite sure, Mammy. He brought this bag of crullers which Aunt Squeaky sent to you."

Mother Graymouse became very anxious when supper was over and still Limpy-toes did not come. She stole into the play-room and looked in every corner. Then bidding Silver Ears rock Squealer to sleep, she hastened down to tell Grand-daddy Whiskers her trouble.

"I fear that some dreadful accident has befallen my poor, dear Limpy-toes," she sobbed.

"Now, Daughter Betsey, don't you worry," was Grand-daddy's cheerful reply. "Limpy-toes is a wise lad and knows well how to look out for himself. I will light my lantern, however, and go out. Perhaps I may meet him."

Mother Graymouse went home somewhat comforted and laden with a pocketful of good things which Granny sent the children from the pantry shelves.

Grand-daddy Whiskers and Uncle Squeaky searched all that evening, flashing their lanterns into every dark corner, but at midnight they had to tell Mother Graymouse that no trace of Limpy-toes was to be found.

Poor Mammy cried and cried. All night long she wondered which enemy had captured her oldest son. Could it be old Thomas Cat? Was he caught in some dreadful trap, or had he eaten poison like poor Daddy? At last she fell asleep.

[Ilustration: My poor, dear Limpy-toes, she sobbed.]

In the morning as she prepared the little bowls of oat-meal, she kept wiping her eyes.

"How shall I ever tell the poor dears that their brother is dead?" she sighed.

At last, Silver Ears, Buster, Tiny and Teenty were seated around the breakfast-table sipping their hot porridge. Mother Graymouse was dressing Baby Squealer who was howling, as usual.

"Where is Limpy-toes, Mammy?" asked Tiny. "Didn't he come home?"

"Sniff! sniff!" went Mother Graymouse. "My poor children, I fear you will never see your dear brother again."

While she was speaking, there came the far-off patter, patter, scratch, scratch, of somebody climbing up to the attic.

"Grand-daddy Whiskers," guessed Mother Graymouse, "or it may be Uncle Squeaky bringing us bad news."

And then, up through the hole in the attic floor, who should appear but Limpy-toes himself!

"Boo-hoo!" cried Baby Squealer as his mother dropped him in a wriggling heap among the cradle pillows and ran to hug Limpy-toes.

"Tell us all about it?" they begged, as Limpy-toes drew up his little stool and asked for his bowl of oat-meal porridge.

"I had quite an adventure," laughed Limpy-toes. "It wasn't so bad, only I knew Mammy would worry. I slipped into the play-room while Silvy got supper, hoping to find something good to eat. That Maid Norah was there and she tried to hit me with an old shoe. I couldn't get back through our holes, but had to run down-stairs. I dodged old Thomas Cat and ran and ran. Ruth Giant opened the door and I whisked out onto the piazza.

19

"At first I thought of going through the subway down to Uncle Squeaky's. But I remembered that our meal-bag was empty. The barn was near and I ran out to fill my pockets in the meal-chest."

"While I was working, Mr. Giant came into the barn and got a dishful of meal for his chickens. It was quite dark and he did not see me. But all at once, down slammed the lid, and there I was, a prisoner for the night! Well, the meal made a soft bed and I slept nicely. This morning, Norah opened the grain chest and I sprang out so swiftly that she hardly saw me. I had a narrow escape from old Thomas Cat, but here I am, safe and sound. Please, Mammy, may I have some more porridge?"

CHAPTER VI.

BUSTER AND THE CHOCOLATES

It was a hot summer day. Mother Graymouse had taken her children out for a stroll in the fields. Only Buster remained at home. He had been naughty and was punished by being left behind.

"I'd rather lie here and read my picture book than trot around in the hot sunshine," he thought. "If only I had some candy, I would be quite happy."

After he had looked at all the pictures and read one of the shortest stories, he shut the book and began to sing softly to himself.

By-and-by he grew restless. "Oh, dear, I'm not one bit sleepy. I can't take another nap. I wish I had some candy. I wonder--"

Then he pushed Baby Squealer's high-chair over to the cupboard and climbed up until he could reach the shelf where Silver Ears had put the Christmas candy. It was gone; every single piece.

"Oh, I know!" remembered Buster. "Ruth Giant had a birthday party last night. I think there may be some candy in the play-room. It will do no harm to look."

He stole softly into the play-room on tiptoe, lest old Thomas Cat might be prowling about and hear him. Ruth Giant was sitting among the pillows upon the couch, reading a book. Beside her was a box of splendid chocolates. Now and then she ate one.

Buster hid behind the doll's dresser and waited. At last he got impatient.

"She will eat 'em all up and I know they are real good," he fussed. "Mammy will come home and call me pretty soon. Oh, why doesn't somebody call Ruth Giant down-stairs? I wonder if she would think I was Silver Ears and toss me some candy? It can't be poison, for she is eating it her own self."

At last, such a long at last, Buster thought, Ruth closed her book and went away. How Buster did hurry to get his greedy little paws into that box of chocolates!

He ran home with one, frisked back for another, and still another, until the very last one of Ruth's fine chocolates was added to the delicious heap on Buster's bed.

"My, but that was hard work!" panted the fat, lazy, little fellow. "I wonder where I can hide 'em so I can have candy to nibble when I want it?"

Down behind an old trunk was a pair of old boots that Mr. Giant had brought to the attic. They were rather musty and dusty, but Buster decided it would be quite safe to hide his candy in one of them. So he trotted back and forth until half of the chocolates were stored away in the toe of a boot.

"I guess I can eat the rest before Mammy comes, for I'm real hungry for candy," thought Buster. He lay down on his little bed and snuggled cosily among the pillows with his book and candy.

"Just like Ruth Giant," he thought proudly, as he nibbled a chocolate. "It is almost as good as having a birthday party of my own. And it is much nicer than tramping around out of doors, if Mammy does call it a picnic."

When Mother Graymouse returned, the children were all eager to tell Buster about their good time in the fields.

"We went down the lane," said Silver Ears, "and found lots of sweet wild flowers."

"And we met Mr. Hop Toad and his wife out for a stroll," added Limpy-toes. "Yes, and we saw Pete and Dickie Grasshopper, and Madame Butterfly, also."

"We had our lunch in a lovely grove of ferns," piped Tiny's shrill little voice.

"It was a lovely, cool grove," echoed Teenty, "and we had a nice lunch."

Buster listened sleepily. Now and then he rubbed his stomach.

"Were you lonely, Buster?" asked his mother.

"No, ma'am."

"Did you have a good nap?"

"Yes, ma'am."

"Are you sick, child?" she demanded, anxiously.

"Yes, Mammy," wailed Buster. "It seems as if my little jacket would burst! Boo-hoo!"

Mother Graymouse hastened to get him a hot drink, but poor Buster rolled and tossed upon his little bed.

Grand-daddy Whiskers came puffing up to the attic with a pan of warm biscuits under his arm. Mother Graymouse looked relieved, for Grand-daddy was quite a doctor.

"What shall I do for the poor child, Grand-daddy?" she asked.

"What has he been eating?" was Grand-daddy's first question as he bent over Buster's bed.

"They weren't poison, Grand-daddy, 'cause Ruth Giant was eating 'em her own self," moaned Buster.

"Eating what?" cried Mammy and Grand-daddy in the same breath.

"Chocolates," confessed Buster.

"How many?" demanded Grand-daddy sternly.

"Only ten," whimpered Buster.

"I will be right back," said Grand-daddy. "There is a bottle of castor oil on the pantry shelf. That was what the doctor gave Robert when he ate too much candy. You will get a good dose, young man, and then you will feel better. Ten chocolates; the greedy little pig!" he grumbled as he hurried away.

"I won't take castor oil, Mammy!" cried Buster. "It tastes horrid."

"You will take castor oil, Buster," replied Mother Graymouse, "if I have to hold your nose."

Grand-daddy soon returned with the oil bottle and in spite of Buster's kicks and squeals, he managed to pour a big dose down his throat.

In a short time, Granny Whiskers came up to see her sick grandchild.

"I fear that oil will not cure him," she said. "You see, he has been eating a good deal of sweet. What he needs is some sour medicine."

She disappeared down the hole and soon returned with a bottle of vinegar tucked under her plaid shawl.

"Aren't you afraid that vinegar will strangle the poor dear?" protested Mother Graymouse.

"Not a bit of it; not a bit of it! Give me a spoon," directed Granny.

Buster made a wry face as he swallowed the sour dose. Then he began to cough and splutter and choke until Mammy grew frightened.

Uncle Squeaky appeared upon the scene just then.

"Stop that, you young rascal!" he laughed. "That is a very poor imitation of a cough. What you need is neither oil nor vinegar, but a good dose of salt. You are altogether too fresh for a youngster."

Buster stopped choking at once. Soon he began to feel better. Then he called Silver Ears.

"There's ten more chocolates hidden in the toe of the Giant's boot, Silvy," he whispered weakly. "Bring 'em out and eat 'em for supper. I'm not hungry for candy any more."

He rolled over and tried to go to sleep. Silver Ears dived down into the boot toe and pulled out the hidden candies. And so the Graymouse family found two plump chocolates at each place when they sat down to supper.

"It has been a lovely picnic day," lisped Tiny, nibbling her chocolate.

"It has been a real lovely day," echoed Teenty sweetly.

Poor Buster, his face hidden in the pillows, remembered his picnic day--chocolate, castor oil, vinegar, and pain,--and he just scowled and scowled.

CHAPTER VII.

SILVER EARS' ADVENTURE

It was a rainy day. Big drops splashed against the window-panes and drummed upon the attic roof.

Silver Ears was restless. She had helped Mammy sweep the floor, had wiped the dishes, and rocked Baby Squealer to sleep. She did not wish to sew any more patchwork squares.

She could hear Ruth Giant laughing softly in the play-room.

"I'd like to be Ruth Giant's pet," she thought wistfully. "That strawberry jam cake was lovely and so were the chocolates and pop-corn. I mean to visit her again. I know Ruth Giant is not an enemy. Mammy need not fear."

She tied her pink ribbon bow under her chin, and without a word to anyone, slipped through a hole into the play-room.

But oh dear me! Ruth Giant had company. A little girl with brown curls and great brown eyes was sitting in Ruth Giant's rocking-chair. Silver Ears hid behind the doll's dresser which stood near the biggest hole. Perhaps Ruth would not want her for a pet to-day. Maybe the other girl would be afraid of a mouse. Some girls were silly just like that. So Silver Ears waited and listened.

"Let's play dinner-party, Dorothy," Ruth was saying. "I like to play dinner-party on rainy days. It is ever so cosy. We must dress the dolls in their prettiest gowns."

The two girls worked busily away putting dainty white dresses upon their flaxen-haired dolls. Silver Ears listened with great interest. She learned that the dark-eyed doll with the red sash was Pansy; Daisy wore a blue ribbon to match her eyes; while the one who was dressed in yellow silk was named Rose.

They were very stylish dolls and wore lace collars, pretty hair ribbons and strings of beads. It took quite a while to get them ready for the party.

"Now if you will spread this napkin on the table, Dorothy, I will go down and coax Norah for some nice things to eat," planned Ruth.

25

Dorothy set the tiny table with a cunning tea-set of white and gold. Then she placed Daisy, Pansy and Rose around the table.

"Oh, isn't it lovely!" cried Ruth. "Just see all the nice things that dear old Norah fixed for us."

She put a plate of cold chicken, some bread and butter sandwiches, a glass of raspberry jam and four frosted cup cakes upon the table.

"How nice!" exclaimed Dorothy. "Oh, I just love dinner parties!"

"So do I," thought Silver Ears. "I wish they would invite me to dinner."

"Dinner is served," announced Ruth, sweetly. "Oh, my! I never thought about something to drink until I saw the empty cups. I must ask Norah to make us some cocoa."

"I'll go down with you," said Dorothy.

"Oh, joy!" Silver Ears almost clapped her excited little paws. Chicken, jam, frosted cake! The minute the play-room door was closed, she invited herself to dinner. Daisy, Pansy and Rose looked smilingly on and said never a word while she nibbled some cake and dipped her paw daintily into the jam. Then she tried the chicken. It was the most delicious chicken she had ever tasted.

"I hope it will take that Norah Maid a long time to make the cocoa," she thought, and her sharp teeth nibbled the chicken as fast as ever they could.

By-and-by, Silver Ears heard footsteps. Seizing a slice of chicken, she whisked softly into the doll's bed and, safely hidden under the blankets, kept on with her feast.

"Now we are all ready at last," laughed Ruth. "I think I must make Tommy sit beside me. He does not behave real good at dinner-parties. I cannot teach him not to put his paws on the table."

Silver Ears began to tremble. So that cross old Tom Cat was a guest at the dinner-party! That cruel, black Tom with the brass eyes and sharp claws. Suppose--just suppose!

"Why, Ruth!" exclaimed Dorothy, "one of the dolls has been eating cake."

"And where in the world is all that chicken?" wondered Ruth. "It is over half gone. Tommy wasn't here or I'd think he was the thief. Who do you suppose could have---"

Ruth paused suddenly to watch Tommy. He was acting strangely. He sniffed at the table, hopped down and ran straight to the doll's bed, like the keen-nosed detective that he was.

Out popped Silver Ears. She darted across the room and squeezed through the tiniest hole just as Tom's sharp claws reached out to grab her. She slipped safely through to the other side and Tom went angrily back to the empty bed, switching his long tail. He had to be content with a piece of cold chicken for his dinner that day.

Silver Ears ran sobbing to Mammy.

"My dear child," said Mother Graymouse, "you are all of a quiver. And your poor little back is bleeding!"

She hurried to find some lint and cobwebs in the dark, unswept corners of the attic.

"Do not be frightened, Silvy. Mammy will fix you up as good as new. Run down to Grand-daddy, Limpy-toes, and fetch a pinch of cure-all salve. By to-morrow, your scratch will be all well, Silvy dear."

"Oh, such a fright!" gasped Silver Ears. "I don't wish to be Ruth Giant's pet any more. She can have her dear Tommy if she wants him."

"Did you get anything good to eat?" asked Buster.

"Oh, yes. Come over here, twinnies, and I will tell you all about it. I wish I'd had time to stuff some of that chicken and frosted cake into my pocket for you all. It was a splendid dinner party, if that old Tom hadn't been invited."

"Chicken, raspberry jam and frosted cake," repeated Buster in his slow, drawling voice. "Say, Silvy, don't you mind that scratch. I'd risk it for such a good feast. Do you suppose there's any left?"

"I forbid you all to enter that play-room again without asking my permission," commanded Mother Graymouse.

"Don't risk it, Buster," laughed Silver Ears. "Why, you never would have reached that hole. You are too fat to run fast. I nearly missed it. And anyway, you would have stuck in the middle of that teentiest hole and old Tom would have chewed your tail right off."

"True, quite true," echoed Mother Graymouse, wagging her head solemnly.

CHAPTER VIII.

VISITING MRS. FIELD-MOUSE

One fine morning in midsummer, Mother Graymouse and her family started upon their annual outing.

Mrs. Field-Mouse, who was a distant cousin of Daddy Graymouse, lived near Pond Lily Lake. Mother Graymouse usually visited her each year in August.

The children had been looking forward to this trip for many days. The bag which had once held the Christmas candy, was packed with dainties for the little Field-Mouse Cousins. Limpy-toes and Buster were to take turns carrying it, while Silver Ears helped her mother with Squealer.

They started quite early in the morning, while the grass was wet with dew, for it was a long walk and by noon the sun would be very hot.

Tiny and Teenty raced merrily on ahead, picking bouquets of wild blossoms and calling gaily to the butterflies and honey bees who were flitting among the flowers.

By-and-by, the tired little party stopped to rest under a clump of red clover. Granny Whiskers had slipped a ginger cookie into each tiny pocket when they called at her door to say good-by. These cookies made a nice luncheon for them.

"How much farther is it, Mammy?" asked Tiny.

"We must follow this crooked path that leads through the sweet clover, then go to the south of a big corn field. Do you see the top of that wild cherry tree over yonder? Well, Cousin Field-Mouse lives near that tree."

They were soon rested and eager to go on. It was sweet among the nodding pink and white clover blossoms. The tall corn stalks, with their silky tassels, seemed like a forest to the timid children, but Mother Graymouse trotted bravely on. Under the shade of the wild cherry tree, however, she paused in confusion.

"Why, Mr. Giant has plowed this land all up for his garden!" she cried. "Poor Cousin Field-Mouse! Her comfortable home has been destroyed."

"Must we go home?" sighed Silver Ears.

"I'm tired," mourned Buster.

"Wait. I see Dickie Grasshopper over by the pond," said Limpy-toes. "Perhaps he can tell us where Cousin Field-Mouse lives now."

Dickie Grasshopper agreed at once to show them the way to Mrs. Field-Mouse's new home. He went on ahead with a hop, skip and jump, so that they had to hurry to keep him in sight. He soon brought them, warm and breathless, to a pile of rails near the corn field.

"I thank you very kindly, Dickie," said Mother Graymouse. Then she knocked upon the door of the humble cottage.

"Why, my dear Betsey!" cried Mrs. Field-Mouse. "I am glad to see you! And all of the children. Dearie sakes, how they do grow! This is a pleasure, a real surprise party. Do come in and take off your bonnet."

"We did not know that you had moved, Debbie," said Mother Graymouse as she untied Squealer's bonnet strings. "How did it happen?"

Tears came into Mrs. Field-Mouse's eyes.

"Oh, it was dreadful, Betsey, just dreadful! One bright, sunshiny morning in the spring, there came a terrible earthquake. All in a minute, our home was a mass of ruins. Pa Field-Mouse was away from home. I snatched Baby Wee and saved him. But oh, my dear Betsey, of all my ten children, Wee and Nimble-toes were the only ones to escape. Sniff! sniff! sniff!"

"Sniff! sniff!" cried Mother Graymouse.

"Well, we mice must make the best of things," added Mrs. Field-Mouse more cheerfully. "Our new home is snug and sheltered and not nearly as damp as the old one. There is an abundance of sweet corn and other juicy vegetables in the Giant's garden, and a big oak tree near by to supply us with all the acorns we shall need for next winter.

"The pond is near, also. Pa Field-Mouse has built us a small raft of dried mushrooms and sometimes we go sailing across the water. Pa and Nimble-toes are down by the pond, gathering seeds. When they come home, Nimble-toes shall show the dear children the sights."

When Pa Field-Mouse and Nimble-toes returned, Mrs. Field-Mouse had dinner ready, out under the oak tree in real picnic fashion. Nimble-toes danced with delight when he saw the bag of rare goodies. Buster, however, thought that the minced turnip and seed salad was a great treat.

Baby Squealer never cried "Boo-hoo!" once all that long summer day. He played with Baby Wee as smiling and happy as could be.

"The darling is always as good as gold when he is out doors," said Mother Graymouse.

"I always said it was fresh air and sunshine that made Wee so healthy," agreed Ma Field-Mouse.

After dinner, Nimble-toes invited Limpy-toes, Silver Ears, Buster and the twins to go out and play with him. They went down to the pond, which was dotted with sweet, white lilies, and watched the fish splash in the water.

Grandpa Bull Frog hopped over to chat with them. He invited them to a frog concert which was to be held that evening.

"We would love to stay," smiled Silver Ears, "but I fear Mammy will go home early."

"Grandpa Bull Frog plays a bass-viol," explained Nimble-toes. "He plays very nicely."

"So does my Uncle Squeaky," bragged Buster, "only he plays a fiddle."

A big black snake crawled along just then and frightened the twins so badly that they all had to run away from the pond.

In the garden, Nimble-toes showed them how to climb a corn-stalk, peel off the husks and nibble the sweet, white kernels.

"Oh, isn't it sweet and juicy!" cried Buster. "Say, Nimble-toes, I'd like to stay here a whole month."

"You would grow fatter than ever," laughed Limpy-toes. "But it is delicious."

They found some little red berries growing under the oak tree, that tasted very much like Uncle Squeaky's checkermints. Nimble-toes said that they were checkerberries.

All too soon, the sun sank in the west, it began to grow dark and Mammy called that it was time to start for home.

It was a fine moonlight evening and the walk home seemed short. Crickets were singing their even-songs all along the road. Whippoor-wills and tree toads shrilled their calls, also. From Pond Lily Lake, they heard faint, sweet sounds in the distance as the frog concert began.

"It has been a lovely day, Mammy," said Silver Ears. "I would like to live away out in the country."

"Where there are sweet, juicy ears of corn," added Buster.

"Nimble-toes promised to take me for a sail some day," said Limpy-toes.

"Oh, let's go again, Mammy," lisped Tiny.

"Let's go," echoed Teenty.

Baby Squealer was sound asleep in the candy bag which hung over Mother Graymouse's shoulder, so he did not even say "Boo-hoo!"

"Well, well, dearies, we did have a delightful visit," replied Mother Graymouse. "Perhaps some day we will go again."

CHAPTER IX.

MOVING DAYS

One day, Mother Graymouse put on her gray bonnet with the blue ribbons on it, and hunted around for the candy bag. She was going shopping. When at last she found the bag, there was a hole in one corner.

"I have not used it since the day we visited Cousin Debbie Field-Mouse," she remembered. "That naughty Baby Squealer must have chewed a hole in it on the way home. Please bring a needle and thread and mend it for me, Silvy."

"There is no thread, Mammy. I used the last needleful yesterday sewing patchwork."

"Dear me, I shall have to get some," sighed Mother Graymouse. "I have a whole paper of needles, but they are useless without thread."

"I saw Ruth Giant making a doll's dress in the play-room," lisped Tiny, "and she had a nice, new spool of white cotton. I didn't go in, Mammy, truly I didn't. Teenty and I were peeping through the littlest hole."

When Mother Graymouse had gone, Silver Ears was eager for another adventure.

"We need that nice new spool of thread," she argued, "and I mean to get it. No, Buster, you are too fat to run fast, and Limpy-toes is lame. I shall not let the twins venture, for old Tom is often in the play-room. So I must go myself."

Away she skipped, before cautious Limpy-toes could say no. Pretty soon she slipped through the tiniest hole, laughing gleefully. She held a long white thread in her mouth.

"Hurry and bring the empty spool," she cried. "I fooled old Tom that time. He was asleep on the couch and never heard me. I couldn't pull the spool through the hole, so I've brought one end of the thread. We'll take turns winding it on to our spool."

They wound, and wound, and wound.

"Seem's if there is no end," complained Buster.

Limpy-toes went on with the work. Suddenly, the thread tightened and the spool in the playroom stopped bobbing.

The twins crept slyly to the hole to see what had happened. They came back giggling softly.

"Old Tom thinks someone is bobbing it for him to play with," lisped Tiny.

"Stop winding," directed Silver Ears, "and old Tom will soon take another nap."

When Mother Graymouse returned, Silver Ears had the shopping bag neatly mended and there was plenty of thread upon their spool.

"I meant to have gone for it myself. And I had told you, Silvy, never to go to the play-room without asking," she scolded.

"I'm sorry I disobeyed, Mammy," said Silver Ears. "You see, we needed the thread so badly and it was such fun to fool old Tom, that I forgot what you said. Please forgive me, Mammy?"

"Yes, dear, I will forgive you this time. But oh, such a risk!" she sighed.

Next day, Silver Ears discovered that all three of the holes into the play-room had been stuffed with yellow soap.

"The nasty tasting stuff!" she scolded. "How can we ever get it out? If we chew new holes, I suppose they will be stuffed, too."

When Mother Graymouse called upon Granny Whiskers, she found her in great trouble.

"The cookies are shut tight in pails. The cheese and meat are covered. The only food in sight is set around on the pantry shelves in traps. The Giants mean to starve us out. Such terrible times as have befallen us!" she moaned.

Uncle Squeaky was of the same opinion. Mr. Giant had been very angry when he found the pumpkin play-house that Wink and Wiggle had made. He found fault because his choice red apples were nibbled.

"And now," continued Uncle Squeaky in a disgusted tone, "the whole cellar is full of traps."

They held a serious counsel,--Grand-daddy and Granny Whiskers, Uncle and Aunt Squeaky, and Mother Graymouse. They talked until midnight. When the clock struck twelve, Grand-daddy summed it all up.

"This has been going on for some time. War is now declared. Our enemies are stronger, wiser and richer than ourselves. Daddy Graymouse has lost his life, Limpy-toes had lost some toes, and I have lost a generous piece out of one ear. We must consider the safety of our children. It is wise, therefore, to retreat before it is too late," he finished, looking very solemn. The other four wagged their heads in approval.

Next morning when all the little Graymouses were eating their breakfast food, Mother Graymouse announced soberly, "My dears, we are going to move."

"Out into the country?" cried Silver Ears and Buster at once.

"Out into the barn."

"Oh, dear!" wailed five little mice.

"Boo-hoo!" cried Baby Squealer.

"Listen, dearies," argued Mammy patiently. "Our lives are no longer safe in this attic. Our enemies are cruel. We must go. But Grand-daddy and Uncle Squeaky will go with us. You will have Dot, Scamper, Wink and Wiggle for playmates. Just think what fun you ten children will have together. Uncle Squeaky knows a snug place in the hay loft where we can live in safety. There's plenty of grain in the barrels and the store is still across the street. We older folk may even venture into the Giant's pantry now and then. But we think it best to take you children out of danger."

"It might be worse," remarked Limpy-toes.

"I shall love to have Cousin Dot with us," smiled Silver Ears.

"And Wink and Wiggle," added the twins.

"Prob'ly Granny will make us some ginger cookies," drawled Buster. "But oh, Mammy, what hard work it will be to move!"

"It will, indeed," agreed Mother Graymouse, "so I think, Buster, that you may as well start right now to help me pack. There's my rocking chair, Squealer's cradle and high-chair, all your little beds and stools, besides my dishes,--it makes me weary just to think of it."

"We must not forget our needles and thread," said Silver Ears. "I mean to rummage in these trunks and get a whole lot of stuff for dresses and bonnets and patchwork. And our shopping bag--we must not forget that."

Each night as it grew dusky, a busy little procession marched to the barn, laden with their household goods. It took a long time, for they meant to stock up as heavily as possible for the coming winter.

But at last, Granny wrapped herself in her plaid shawl, slipped a bottle of castor oil and another of vinegar into her skirt pocket, and said good-by to her pantry home. Uncle Squeaky, with his precious fiddle tucked under his arm, joined her and Grand-daddy. Then followed Mother Graymouse and her little brood, with Aunt Squeaky and the cousins.

But the next week was Thanksgiving. Granny, Mammy and Aunt Squeaky were good cooks and they forgot their sadness in their preparations to celebrate the holiday. And so it was a jolly, thankful party which sat down to the feast at Grand-daddy Whisker's long table which was laden with good things for their Thanksgiving dinner.

CHAPTER X.

THE CHRISTMAS TREE

It was twilight time. Silver Ears, Dot and Buster were sitting in the fragrant hay. Over in another corner of the loft, Wink and Wiggle were playing a game of tag with the Graymouse twins.

"Let's have a Christmas tree next week, like the young Giants did last year," proposed Silver Ears.

"All trimmed with pop-corn and candy!" exclaimed Buster. "Oh, Silvy, that would be grand!"

"Let's go right now and find Scamper and Limpy-toes," said Dot. "We will ask them to help us choose a tree and bring it home. There is lovely moon-light, out of doors."

Mother Graymouse and Aunt Squeaky said they might go to the woods if they would be very careful. So they dressed warmly and started out.

They met Limpy-toes and Scamper dragging home the shopping bag filled with delicious cream cheese from the store.

They readily agreed to help find a tree. Limpy-toes led the way. He remembered seeing a pretty little cedar tree down by the pond when they had visited Cousin Field-Mouse.

It was a long walk, but at last they found it, all powdered with snow which sparkled in the moonlight.

Such a frolic! They took turns hacking away at it with their tiny hatchet, giving merry squeals when the cedar twigs pricked their paws. Then they dragged it home, making a funny path in the snow.

"To-morrow we will come again," planned Scamper, "and we will bring Wink and Wiggle, Teenty and Tiny. We must all gather princess pine, evergreen and holly to trim the barn so it will look real Christmasy."

All that week, the children had a jolly time. They made holly wreaths dotted with red berries, and yards of evergreen trimming. Grand-daddy set the cedar tree in one corner where it looked very grand.

Uncle Squeaky slipped into the Giant's pantry one evening, when his keen nose smelled pop-corn, and came back with a load of the fluffy white stuff.

"Get your needles, children," called Mother Graymouse, "and we will string some pop-corn for the tree."

They sat in a circle upon the barn floor around the heap of corn and sewed it into strings which Granny Whiskers tossed upon the branches of their tree. Granny was as interested as the youngsters in the Christmas doings.

Another evening, Uncle Squeaky brought home some peppermints and checkermints.

"Here, kiddies, sew some thread through these candies and hang 'em on your tree," he grinned.

"Oh, how pretty!" cried Dot, when the pink and white candies were swinging among the green branches.

At last came Christmas Eve.

"We have a Christmas tree and it is all trimmed lovely," lisped Tiny, "but do you s'pose there'll be any presents like Ruth and Robert Giant had on their tree?"

"They say that Santa comes down from the North Pole on his sled drawn by swift reindeer and brings a great pack filled with presents for good little mice," said Grand-daddy.

"But you must all go to bed early, for he would not want you peeping while he trimmed your tree," added Granny.

It was not easy to go to sleep on Christmas Eve. But at last, Baby Squealer stopped squealing; the twins giggled themselves to the Land of Nod; Wink and Wiggle could not keep their heavy eyes open any longer; and the four oldest children went sound asleep, for they had worked hard that day cracking nuts for Mammy's cake and seeding raisins for Aunt Squeaky's Christmas pudding.

When the clock struck eleven, strange to say, it was Buster's eyes which were still wide open. He was usually very sleepy, but to-night he was very curious. He wanted to see Santa trim that tree. So he winked and he blinked under his blankets, keeping real still and pretending to be asleep.

And what do you think? Grand-daddy began to hang pieces of cheese on the tree! Aunt Squeaky tiptoed in with a pile of cute little hemstitched handkerchiefs; Mammy had a handful of gay ribbon bows and neckties; and Granny was hanging up ten pair of scarlet mittens. Uncle Squeaky brought in a red double-runner sled and pushed it under the tree!

"I guess Santa is a joke," chuckled Buster sleepily. "Won't we have fun sliding on that double-runner Uncle has made!"

Quite happy, he closed his eyes and went sound asleep.

He awoke suddenly when the clock struck one. There was a jingle of sleigh bells; the reindeer were racing across the frozen snow; and there, in the bright moonlight, was old Santa trimming their tree!

Buster gazed in wonder while the fat old fellow tied on handkerchiefs, red mittens, cream cheese, ribbon bows and candies. Why, he was even pushing a sled under the tree!

"That is queer," thought Buster drowsily.

Bright and early next morning, ten little mice were dancing about their tree. Sure enough, Buster found it loaded with the very presents he expected.

"Grand-daddy, did you trim our tree, or did Santa?" he demanded.

"Why do you ask such funny questions, Buster Boy?" laughed Grand-daddy. Then Buster told all he had seen in the night.

"You must have eaten too much cheese for supper," chuckled Uncle Squeaky. "Cheese always makes me dream."

"But did I dream about Santa, or about you and Grand-daddy and Mammy?" insisted Buster.

"Well, that's the question," grinned Uncle Squeaky as he walked off, leaving Buster very much puzzled.

They left the presents on their tree all Christmas day. In the evening, they held a concert.

Uncle Squeaky played upon his fiddle and Buster sang his newest song:

"We are merry as can be,

Happy little mice,
Gathered round our Christmas tree
Hung with gifts so nice.
Jolly little mice are we,
Happy all day long;
So we shout and sing with glee
Our glad Christmas song."

Then Grand-daddy played Santa and distributed the gifts.

"Oh, I think the hay loft is nicer than our attic home, after all," laughed Silver Ears.

"So it is," agreed Limpy-toes.

"Because we are all living together," said Dot.

"I think we have nicer things to eat," drawled Buster.

"And we love to play with Wink and Wiggle," lisped Tiny.

"Yes, my children, it is indeed a Merry Christmas this year," said Grand-daddy. "We are safe and snug in a comfortable home with plenty to eat. I just heard that our old enemy, Thomas Cat, has been run over by Mr. Giant's automobile. He will worry us no more. Your uncle and I are making a profound study of traps. We no longer fear them, because we understand them.

"Come, Uncle Squeaky, tune up and we will all dance around the Christmas tree and sing Buster's new song with right good will."

The jolly old moon, peering through the one dusty window-pane, saw a frolicsome circle of mice join hands and dance around a little cedar tree. They were singing merrily:

"Jolly little mice are we,
Happy all day long;
So we shout and sing with glee
Our glad Christmas song."

And so ended a merry Christmas day in the Giant's barn loft.

Made in the USA
Las Vegas, NV
15 August 2021